EARTH & ME
OUR FAMILY TREE

NATURE'S CREATURES

ONE OF THREE BOOKS
CELEBRATING THE HUMAN RELATION WITH
NATURE'S FEATURES,
NATURE'S CREATURES,
AND NATURE'S PAST AND FUTURE

BY J. PATRICK LEWIS • ILLUSTRATIONS BY CHRISTOPHER CANYON

DAWN PUBLICATIONS

DEDICATIONS

For Peggy Gifford and Jack Fitzpatrick — JPL

For Ted & Betsy—truly joyful friends — CC

Copyright © 2002 J. Patrick Lewis
Illustrations copyright © 2002 Christopher Canyon

A Sharing Nature With Children Book

Library of Congress Cataloging-in-Publication Data

Lewis, J. Patrick.
    Earth & me, our family tree : nature's creatures / by J. Patrick
Lewis ; illustrations by Christopher Canyon.— 1st ed.
       p. cm. — (Sharing nature with children book)
    Summary: Many diverse creatures, including a beetle, a hawk, a
whale, a dragonfly, a deer, a penguin, and a boy, converse about their
habitats, which are all so different, but together make up the Earth.
    ISBN 1-58469-030-5 (pbk.) — ISBN 1-58469-031-3 (hardback)
    [1. Nature—Fiction. 2. Animals—Fiction.]   I. Title: Earth and
me, our family tree. II. Canyon, Christopher, ill. III. Title. IV.
Series.
    PZ7.L5866 Ear 2002
    [E]—dc21
                                    2001004054

Dawn Publications
P.O. Box 2010
Nevada City, CA 95959
530-478-0111
nature@dawnpub.com

Published in Japan by Mikuni Publishing, Tokyo.
Printed in China

10 9 8 7 6 5 4 3 2 1
First Edition

Design and computer production by Andrea Miles

The Beetle listened to his friend,
The Boy who boasted when he said,
"How wonderful to be the best
In all the world—and leap ahead!"

The Boy tried hard to understand
The Beetle, who click-click replied,
"How wonderful are all the rest
Of us, except for human pride."

EARTH

Said the Beetle: "Millions of years ago, we arrived on Earth. Thousands of insect species have lived in, on, and above the planet for centuries. Can humans do the same?"

Said the Boy: "The wisest of my elders all agree that Humans are only newcomers, Beetle. Be patient with us. We must learn how to live peacefully and respectfully on this fragile planet."

And together they looked up to the

SKY

Said the Crane:
"Wind-whisperer, the Sky is
lent to all of Earth's creatures only
for a short time. We are born, we die.
In between, the Sky invites us home, and we
repay the Sky with song."

Said the Hummingbird: "You are a wise bird, Pond-walker. A message for all is that we do the Sky no harm. But birds like us go even further. We leave this high house as clean and clear as we found it, and our wings are things of beauty and grace."

And together they flew near the

SEA

Said the Blue Whale: "Eight-legs, they say that I am bigger
than twenty-six elephants, and six men could carry my
glad heart. Yet it's odd, isn't it?
When I sail down the long night of the sea, I eat only the
tiny krill."

Said the Octopus: "Gentle Water Giant, you are as
graceful as a cloud, and I'm sure your song can be heard
half way to China. But even you are only a speck and a
spectator in the vastness of the Sea."

And together they swam near the

RIVER

Said the Frog: "Welcome home to the upstream, Fatfish! You must be exhausted after swimming hundreds of miles, heavy with several thousand eggs."

Said the Salmon: "I give my whole heart to one goal, Croaker. Just getting to this stream has been my passion. While I was away, did you sing the River your peaceful nightsong? Did you watch the littlest creatures celebrating the ways of water?"

And together they paddled into the

LAKE

Said the Turtle: "I may be one of the slowest creatures on Earth, Glasswing, but isn't that the best way to observe what's passing by? Very slowly? I think I'll take a holiday in my Lake resort.

Said the Dragonfly: "Yes, you are lucky by nature. Patience is your virtue, Roundhat. Speed is mine. I can skim the Lake, race the wind, and be back in time to have a chat with you. And to fly above the Lake, ah, what a reflection on life!"

And together they were humbled by the

MOUNTAIN

Said the Mountain Lion: "You and I are enemies, Cliff-hanger, so watch your step. Yet we would not trade places with anyone for we can spend our entire lives on top of the Earth."

Said the Longhorn Sheep:
"The Mountain doesn't care that
you are sly and I am shy, Lightfoot,
or that you are cunning and I am
cautious. We share this magnificent
rocky home. What better place to watch
the world go by?"

And from separate peaks, they listened to the

VOLCANO

Said the Hawk: "The Volcano is sleeping now, Little Leaper. You never know when she will lose her temper. So hide yourself well. Oh, and by the way, my dinner time is coming soon."

Said the Mouse Hare: "Skywatcher, I sometimes feel the Volcano's anger rumbling through my little body. That's when I know to build my family a new home—and to shy away from you too."

And together they circled around—one in the sky, one on the ground—to the

WOODLAND

Said the Deer: "You are courage without fear, Bigfoot, here in the secrecy of timber. Humans marvel at us and our home from afar. We must be the guardians of the forest."

Said the Bear: "You are humility at a gallop, Night-whisperer. The Woodland loves its quiet creatures too. How wonderful to see you in Earth's natural home of silence and awe."

And together they remembered their friends in the

RAINFOREST

Said the Gorilla: "The rich wet treetops provide us with necessity and luxury, Slitherer. Our babies sway in the canopy, our relatives picnic at ease. Do you ever wonder how we would live without the Rainforest?"

Said the Snake: "I curl up under damp leaves of shelter, Silverback. Sometimes I am awakened by the stirrings of 'progress.' In our evergreen kingdom, I learn by turns. Happily, I know just when to loosen up."

And together they imagined life in the

WETLANDS

Said the Alligator: "I'm wondering what
to have for supper, Stick-leg. Eating is
my life, you know. Hmmm. Maybe I'll just wait
here for something delicious to swim by."

Said the Heron: "You're wondering
about tonight's supper, Whiptail?!
What I'd like to know is whether
these rich bog meadows
of ours will last for
another million years?"

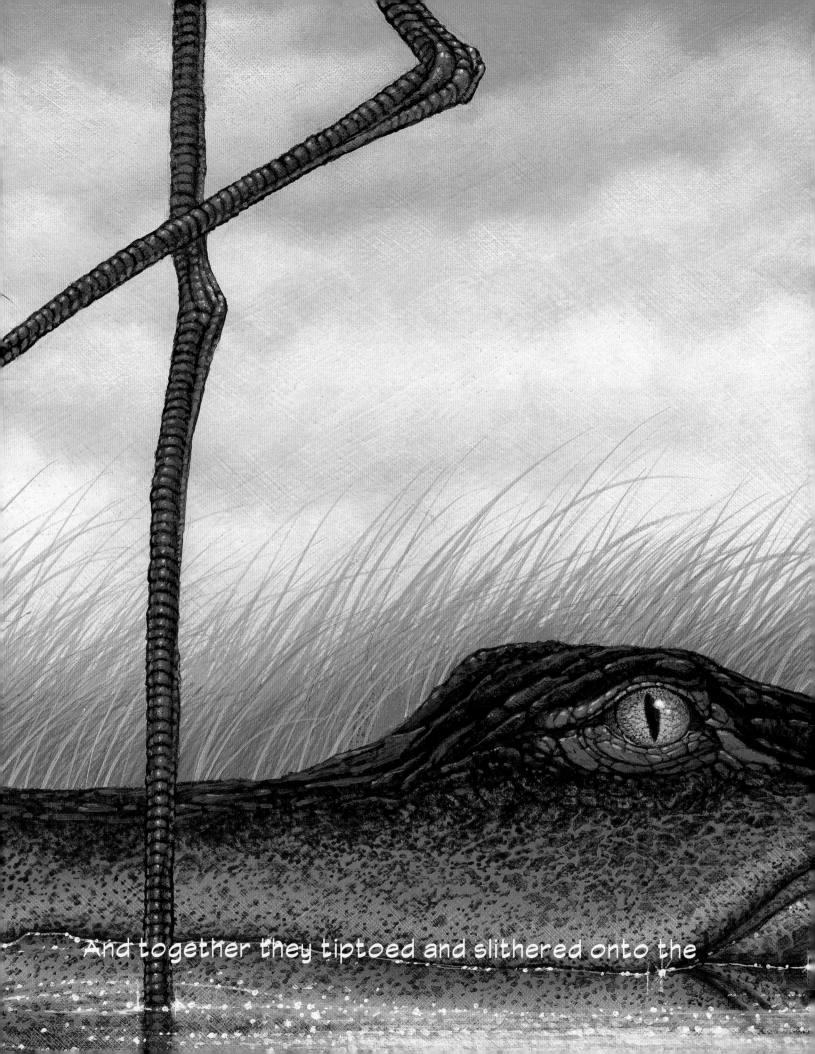

And together they tiptoed and slithered onto the

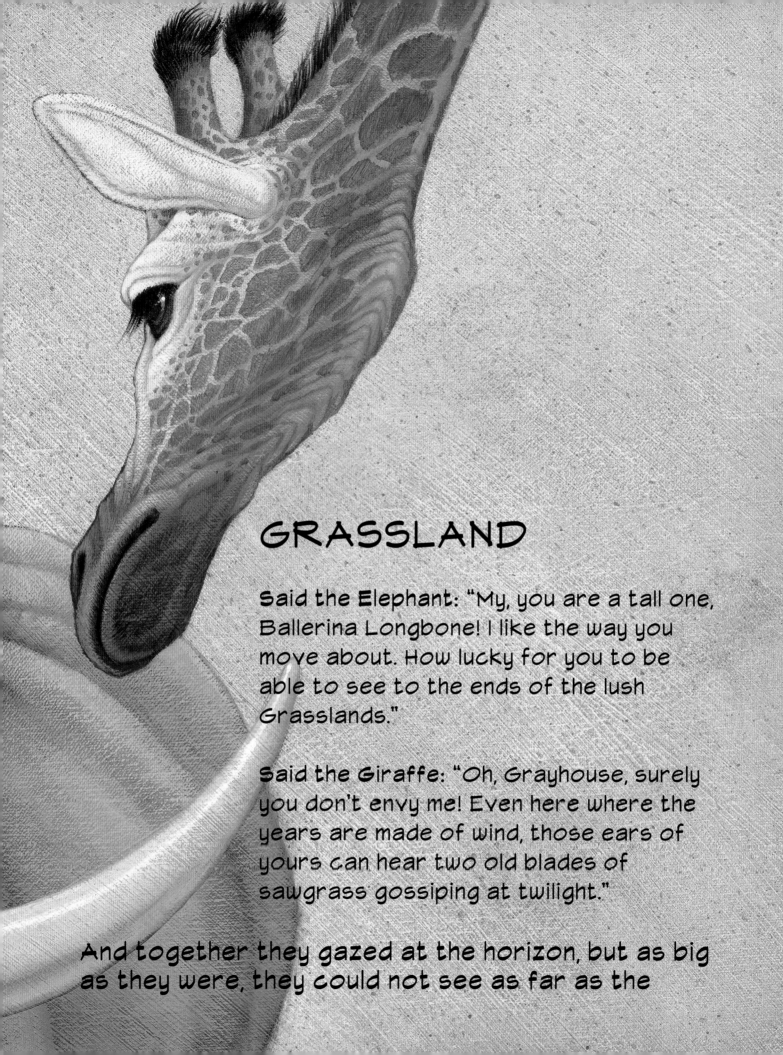

GRASSLAND

Said the Elephant: "My, you are a tall one, Ballerina Longbone! I like the way you move about. How lucky for you to be able to see to the ends of the lush Grasslands."

Said the Giraffe: "Oh, Grayhouse, surely you don't envy me! Even here where the years are made of wind, those ears of yours can hear two old blades of sawgrass gossiping at twilight."

And together they gazed at the horizon, but as big as they were, they could not see as far as the

ICE LAND

Said the Penguin: "The Earth above is white, the Earth below is black, Slick-body. We can move so smoothly and swiftly through the darkness."

Said the Seal: "Animals who live above ground miss the wonders of the deep. Listen, Upstander, there is nothing quite like the sound of water music."

And together they came up for air far, far away from the

HOT LAND

Said the Lizard: "Good morning, Cousin Busybody. Where are you off to today? Filling up the ant pantry? Say, did you notice the Sun singing a song in the Land of Little Rains?"

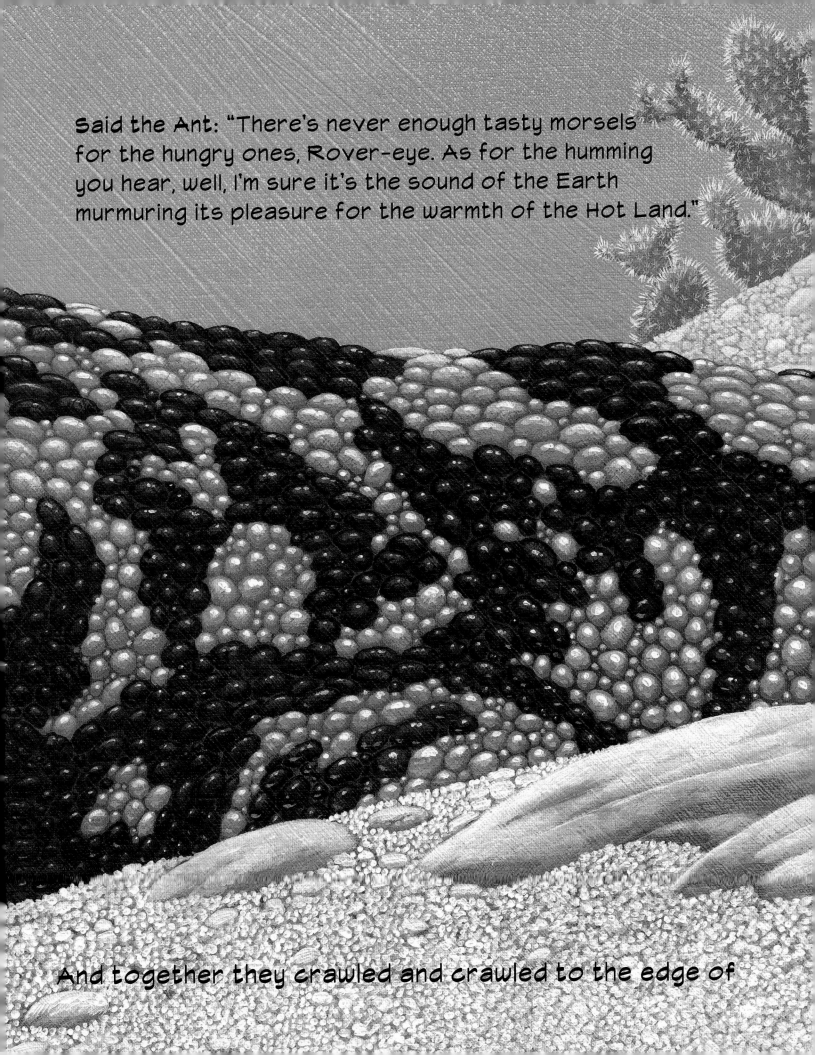

Said the Ant: "There's never enough tasty morsels for the hungry ones, Rover-eye. As for the humming you hear, well, I'm sure it's the sound of the Earth murmuring its pleasure for the warmth of the Hot Land."

And together they crawled and crawled to the edge of

TOWN

Said the Dog: "Aren't you cat-happy, Purr, that Humans built a Town? Just the place for a Mouser like you to discover a little mystery and mischief. Now we can settle down and live peacefully, except of course for my occasional bark and your irritating meow!"

Said the Cat: "Humans must be delighted with loyal dogs like you. But believe me, Barker, someday Cats will receive a special reward because it takes all of a Cat's good manners to live with you in the same Town!"

And together they sniffed around the

SCHOOL

Said the Student: "Tell me, Mrs. Hashimoto, do you think animals can teach us anything about life?"

Said the Teacher: "Animals are like the elders, Naomi. They have the wisdom of experience. No one can teach you everything. But as you walk slowly through time, pay attention to the lessons taught by all of those around you."

And together the Student and the Teacher spun a globe of the

EARTH

Said the Beetle: "You Humans are strong and clever, Boy. You seem to know so much! I wonder, though, if you are wise enough to realize the limitations of your own strength."

Said the Boy : "Humans say that knowledge is power, Beetle, but you're right, it is no substitute for the wisdom of the whole community in which we live.   The road ahead is as mysterious and   uncertain as the long trail we already   have crossed."

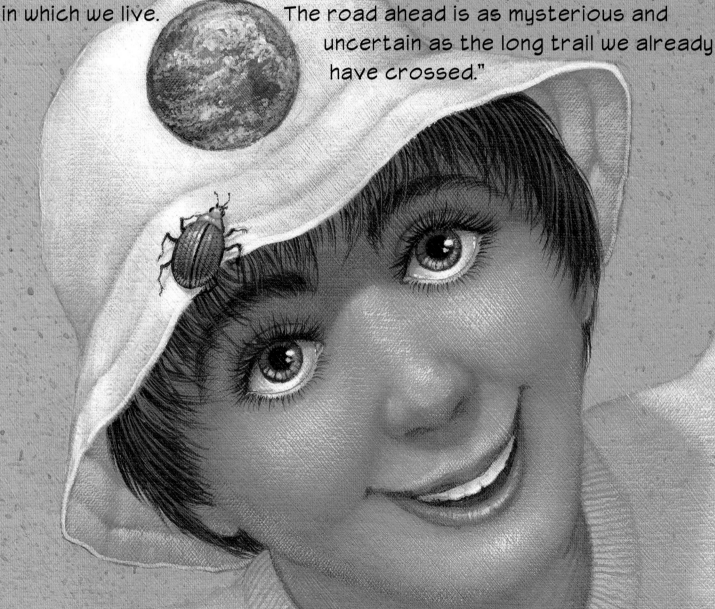

And together the Beetle and the Boy
walked on and on, two creatures among the many
on the smooth and the wrinkled skin of Earth.

For 30 years J. Patrick Lewis was a college professor, teaching economics. Now he plays with words and hangs out with kids at elementary schools. He is out to prove that "poetry is ear candy," and to inspire a simpatico connection with the natural wonders that surround us. "If there is a better way to spend a lifetime," he says, "I can't imagine what it would be." This is his third book with Dawn Publications.

Christopher Canyon is irrepressibly playful as well as passionate about illustrating children's picture books. He teaches illustration at the Columbus College of Art & Design in Columbus, Ohio, is a frequent speaker at professional events, and his illustrations have been displayed in several national exhibitions. But his favorite audience is children and he makes a point of visiting schools often. Two of his previous books for Dawn Publications, **The Tree in the Ancient Forest** and **Stickeen: John Muir and the Brave Little Dog**, won the Benjamin Franklin Award as best illustrated children's books of the year.

THE EARTH TRILOGY
BY J. PATRICK LEWIS, ILLUSTRATED BY CHRISTOPHER CANYON

Earth & You—A Closer View: Nature's Features
Earth & Us—Continuous: Nature's Past and Future
Earth & Me—A Family Tree: Nature's Creatures

OTHER BOOKS ILLUSTRATED BY CHRISTOPHER CANYON

A Tree in the Ancient Forest, by Carol Reed-Jones, demonstrates how interdependent are the plants and animals around a grand old fir.

Stickeen: John Muir and the Brave Little Dog by John Muir as retold by Donnell Rubay. In this classic true story, the relationship between the great naturalist and a small dog is changed forever by their adventure on a glacier in Alaska.

Wonderful Nature, Wonderful You, by Karin Ireland, shows how nature is a great teacher, reminding us to bloom where we are planted— suggesting, with a light touch, how humans might follow nature's example.

A SAMPLING OF NATURE AWARENESS BOOKS FROM DAWN PUBLICATIONS

Born with a Bang: The Universe Tells Our Cosmic Story, by Jennifer Morgan. A first person account, as told by the Universe, of a truly Great Story—its birth at the beginning of time through the formation of Earth. In this first of a series of three, time after time the Universe nearly perishes, but it bravely triumphs and turns itself into something new and even more spectacular—you.

Birds in Your Backyard by Barbara Herkert, is an excellent tool to help kindle the spark of interest in birds at an early age, and so establish a life-long passion for nature in general, and birds in particular.

Under One Rock: Bugs, Slugs and other Ughs by Anthony Fredericks. No child will be able to resist looking under a rock after reading this rhythmic, engaging story—a perfect balance of fact, fiction, and fun.

Salmon Stream, by Carol Reed-Jones, follows the life cycle of salmon, who hatch in a stream, travel the world, and return to their birthplace against staggering odds.

Girls Who Looked Under Rocks, by Jeannine Atkins. Six girls, from the 17th to the 20th century, didn't run from spiders or snakes but crouched down to take a closer look. They became pioneering naturalists, passionate scientists, and energetic writers or artists.

John Muir: My Life with Nature, by Joseph Cornell. John Muir's joyous enthusiasm for nature is contagious in this telling, mostly in his own words, of his remarkable adventures with nature.

Dawn Publications is dedicated to inspiring in children a deeper understanding and appreciation for all life on Earth. To view our full list of titles or order, please visit our web site at www.dawnpub.com, or call 800-545-7475.